Who Built the Stable?

A Nativity Poem by Ashley Bryan

Atheneum Books for Young Readers
NEW YORK LONDON TORONTO SYDNEY NEW DELHI

atheneum

ATHENEUM BOOKS FOR YOUNG READERS
An imprint of Simon & Schuster Children's Publishing Division
1230 Avenue of the Americas, New York, New York 10020
Copyright © 2012 by Ashley Bryan
ATHENEUM BOOKS FOR YOUNG READERS is a registered trademark of
Simon & Schuster, Inc.
Atheneum logo is a trademark of Simon & Schuster Inc.
For information about special discounts for bulk purchases, please
contact Simon & Schuster Special Sales at
1-866-506-1949 or business@simonandschuster.com.
The Simon & Schuster Speakers Bureau can bring authors to your live event.
For more information or to book an event, contact the Simon & Schuster Speakers
Bureau at 1-866-248-3049 or visit our website at www.simonspeakers.com.
The text for this book is set in Howlett.
The illustrations for this book are rendered in tempera and acrylic.
Manufactured in China
0712 SCP
First Edition
2 4 6 8 10 9 7 5 3 1
Library of Congress Cataloging-in-Publication Data
Bryan, Ashley.
Who built the stable? / Ashley Bryan. – 1st ed.
p.   cm.
Summary: A shepherd boy apprenticed to his carpenter father builds
a stable and then welcomes two weary travelers from Nazareth.
ISBN 978-1-4424-0934-7 (hardcover)
ISBN 978-1-4424-5458-3 (eBook)
1. Jesus Christ—Nativity—Juvenile fiction. [1. Stories in rhyme.
2. Jesus Christ—Nativity—Fiction.] I. Title.
PZ8.3.B8286Wh 2012
[E]–dc23   2012010647

For Sister Sheila Flynn and
her Kopanang Women's Group
of Embroiderers,
Geluksdal, South Africa,
my dear creative friends.

Love,
Long Papa Ashley

Who built the stable
Where the Baby Jesus lay?

Was it built of bricks,
Was it built of clay?

Was it built of wooden sticks,

Was it built of sod?

Was it made by human hands,

Was it built by God?

A child built the stable.
A little shepherd boy

Apprenticed as a carpenter
In his father's employ.

He built the wooden stable
For his donkey, ox, and sheep,

A shelter from the weather,
A home at night for sleep.

He watered them at sunrise
Where they'd graze and freely roam.

He called to them at sunset—
"Follow me!"—and led them home.

Was Jesus born in Italy,
Russia, Spain, Japan?

No! He was born in Bethlehem,
A rich and verdant land.

How did Joseph and pregnant Mary
Find a place to stay,

When they went knock knock knocking
And were always turned away?

The little shepherd sheltered them.
For one night he saw a star,

And—Lo!—it grew in brightness,
Approaching from afar.

He looked about in wonder
As there came into his sight,

A poor man and a woman,
Wandering in the night.

The boy asked, "Can I help you?"
Gently Mary spoke to him.

"My child will soon be born," she said.
"There's no room at the inn."

"Oh, come with me!" the boy exclaimed.
"My stable's a warm place.

"My animals will welcome you,
I'll sweep and clear a space."

He made a bin the cradle
Of straw and new-mown hay,

And when at dawn the child was born . . .

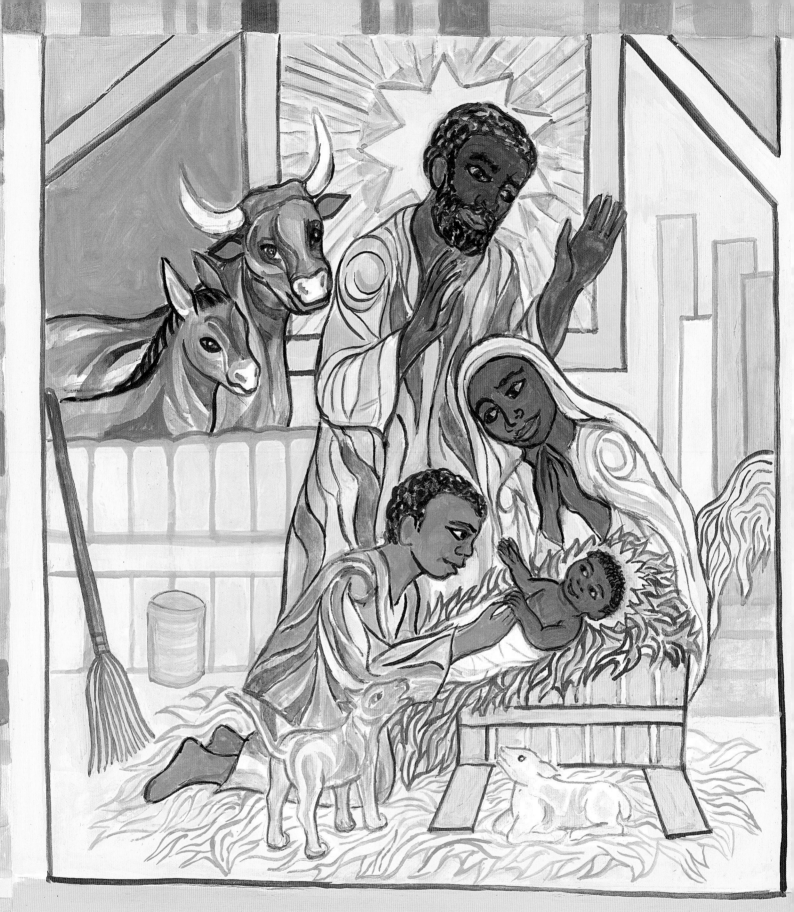

He in the manger lay. The boy looked in
The infant's eyes and in his heart he knew:

The babe would be a carpenter.
He'd be a shepherd too.

Who Built the Stable?
A Nativity Poem

Who built the stable
Where the Baby Jesus lay?
Was it built of bricks,
Was it built of clay?

Was it built of wooden sticks,
Was it built of sod?
Was it made by human hands,
Was it built by God?

A child built the stable.
A little shepherd boy
Apprenticed as a carpenter
In his father's employ.

He built the wooden stable
For his donkey, ox, and sheep,
A shelter from the weather,
A home at night for sleep.

He watered them at sunrise
Where they'd graze and freely roam.
He called to them at sunset—
"Follow me!"—and led them home.

Was Jesus born in Italy,
Russia, Spain, Japan?
No! He was born in Bethlehem,
A rich and verdant land.

How did Joseph and pregnant Mary
Find a place to stay,
When they went knock knock knocking
And were always turned away?

The little shepherd sheltered them.
For one night he saw a star,
And—Lo!—it grew in brightness,
Approaching from afar.

He looked about in wonder
As there came into his sight,
A poor man and a woman,
Wandering in the night.

The boy asked, "Can I help you?"
Gently Mary spoke to him.
"My child will soon be born," she said.
"There's no room at the inn."

"Oh, come with me!" the boy exclaimed.
"My stable's a warm place.
My animals will welcome you,
I'll sweep and clear a space."

He made a bin the cradle
Of straw and new-mown hay,
And when at dawn the child was born . . .
He in the manger lay.

The boy looked in the infant's eyes
And in his heart he knew:
The babe would be a carpenter.
He'd be a shepherd too.